HEROES
AT HOME
SPIDER-MAN

Active Dry
Yeast

HEROES AT HOME
BLACK PANTHER

DINING HALL

MASKS REQUIRED

Must stay 6 ft apart!

6 ft

HEROES
AT HOME
CAPTAIN AMERICA

HEROES
AT HOME
CAPTAIN
MARVEL

THE GALAXY ISN'T BIG ENOUGH FOR THE BOTH OF US!

YOU MAY TRY TO VANQUISH ME, BUT I WON'T MAKE IT EASY.

I WOULDN'T HAVE IT ANY OTHER WAY!

THEN IT BEGIN--
SORRY I'M LATE!

THE DIFFERENT TIME ZONES ARE KILLING ME.
THIS ONLY WORKS IF WE ALL TAKE IT SERIOUSLY!

I AM! I DECLARE MY INTENTION TO FIGHT YOU BOTH TO THE DEATH...JUST AS SOON AS THAT'S A SAFE AND RESPONSIBLE THING TO DO.

WE BETTER WRAP THIS UP-- I DON'T HAVE A PREMIUM ACCOUNT.

WAIT...THOSE STARS ARE SOME KIND OF BACKDROP!
WHERE ARE YOU?

DON'T WORRY ABOUT IT!
J

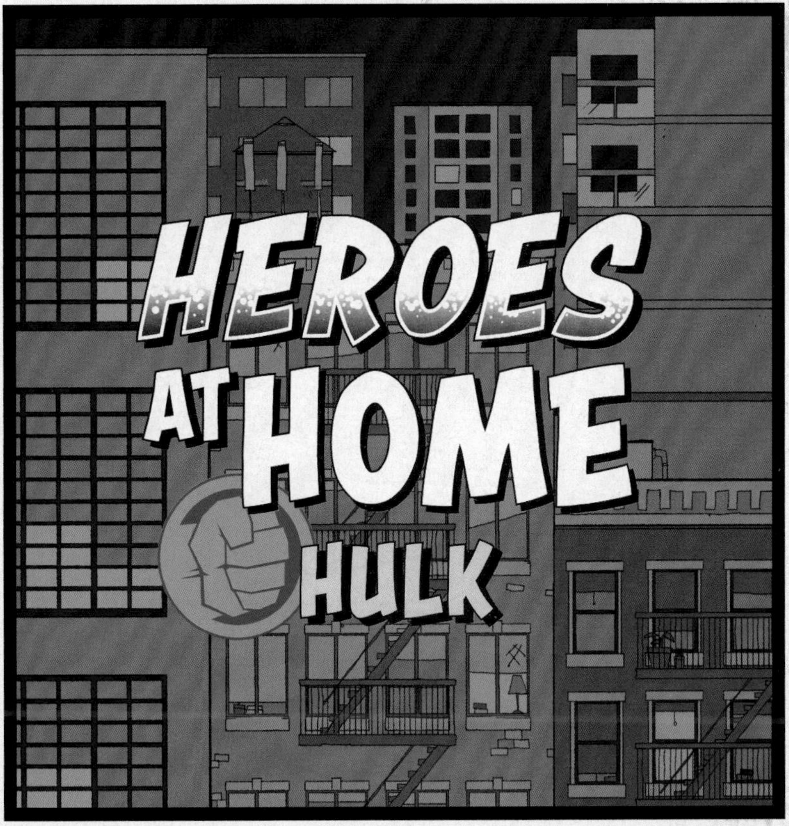
HEROES
AT HOME
HULK

THANK YOU!
ESSENTIAL
WORKERS!
THANK YOU!

THANK YOU
THANK YOU
HEROES
LOVE

WORKERS

HULK SORRY.

HEROES
AT HOME
THOR

SNIP
SNIP
SNIP

SNIP
SNI

SNIP
SNIP
SNIP

SNIP
SNIP
SNIP

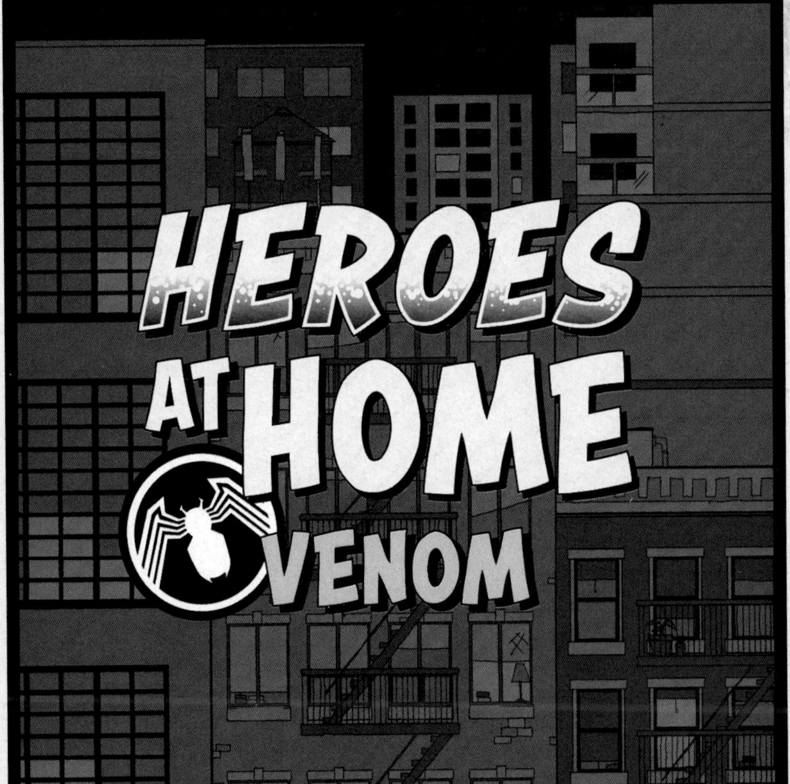
HEROES AT HOME
VENOM

MASK

HEROES
AT HOME
WOLVERINE

For everyone's safety, SHELTER IN PLACE.